# GUARDIANS OF THE GALAXY

# ROCKET RACCOON™ #4

## A CHASING TALE PART FOUR

MARVEL
marvelkids.com
© MARVEL

ABDO
Spotlight

**ABDOPUBLISHING.COM**

Reinforced library bound edition published in 2018 by Spotlight,
a division of ABDO, PO Box 398166, Minneapolis, Minnesota 55439.
Spotlight produces high-quality reinforced library bound editions for
schools and libraries. Published by agreement with Marvel Characters, Inc.

Printed in the United States of America, North Mankato, Minnesota.
042017
092017

THIS BOOK CONTAINS
RECYCLED MATERIALS

marvelkids.com
© 2017 MARVEL

## PUBLISHER'S CATALOGING IN PUBLICATION DATA

Names: Young, Skottie, author. | Young, Skottie ; Beaulieu, Jean-Francois ; Parker,
    Jake, illustrators.
Title: Rocket Raccoon / writer: Skottie Young ; art: Skottie Young ; Jean-Francois
    Beaulieu ; Jake Parker.
Description: Reinforced library bound edition. | Minneapolis, Minnesota : Spotlight,
    2018. | Series: Guardians of the galaxy : Rocket Raccoon | Volumes 1, 2, 3, and
    4 written by Skottie Young ; illustrated by Skottie Young & Jean-Francois
    Beaulieu. | Volumes 5 and 6 written by Skottie Young ; illustrated by Skottie
    Young , Jake Parker & Jean-Francois Beaulieu.
Summary: Rocket's high-flying life of adventure is at stake when he's framed for
    murder, and with an imposter one step ahead of him, and various terminators
    tracking him, can Rocket make it out alive and clear his name?
Identifiers: LCCN 2017931597 | ISBN 9781532140846 (#1: A Chasing Tale Part
    One) | ISBN 9781532140853 (#2: A Chasing Tale Part Two) | ISBN
    9781532140860 (#3: A Chasing Tale Part Three) | ISBN 9781532140877 (#4: A
    Chasing Tale Part Four) | ISBN 9781532140884 (#5: Storytailer) | ISBN
    9781532140891 (#6: Misfit Mechs)
Subjects: LCSH: Superheroes--Juvenile fiction. | Adventure and adventurers--
    Juvenile fiction. | Comic books, strips, etc.--Juvenile fiction. | Graphic novels--
    Juvenile fiction.
Classification: DDC 741.5--dc23
LC record available at https://lccn.loc.gov/2017931597

**Spotlight**

A Division of ABDO
abdopublishing.com

MARVEL ENTERTAINMENT PROUDLY PRESENTS

# ROCKET

GUARDIAN OF THE GALAXY, GUNSLINGER, VICTIM OF IDENTITY THEFT?!

ROCKET HAS ALWAYS THOUGHT HE WAS THE LAST OF HIS KIND, BUT IT LOOKS LIKE ANOTHER RACCOON IS OUT THERE KILLING PEOPLE AND ROCKET JUST WON'T STAND FOR IT.

DIGGING FOR INFO ON THE IMPOSTER, AND WITH A GROUP OF KILLER EX-GIRLFRIENDS ON HIS (BEAUTIFULLY MAINTAINED) TAIL, ROCKET ARRANGED A SIT-DOWN WITH AN INTERGALACTIC KINGPIN KNOWN AS FUNTZEL TO SEE IF HE KNEW ANYTHING.

THE OTHER RACCOON WAS ALREADY THERE, THOUGH, AND - WHAT'S WORSE - HE'S KIDNAPPED GROOT!

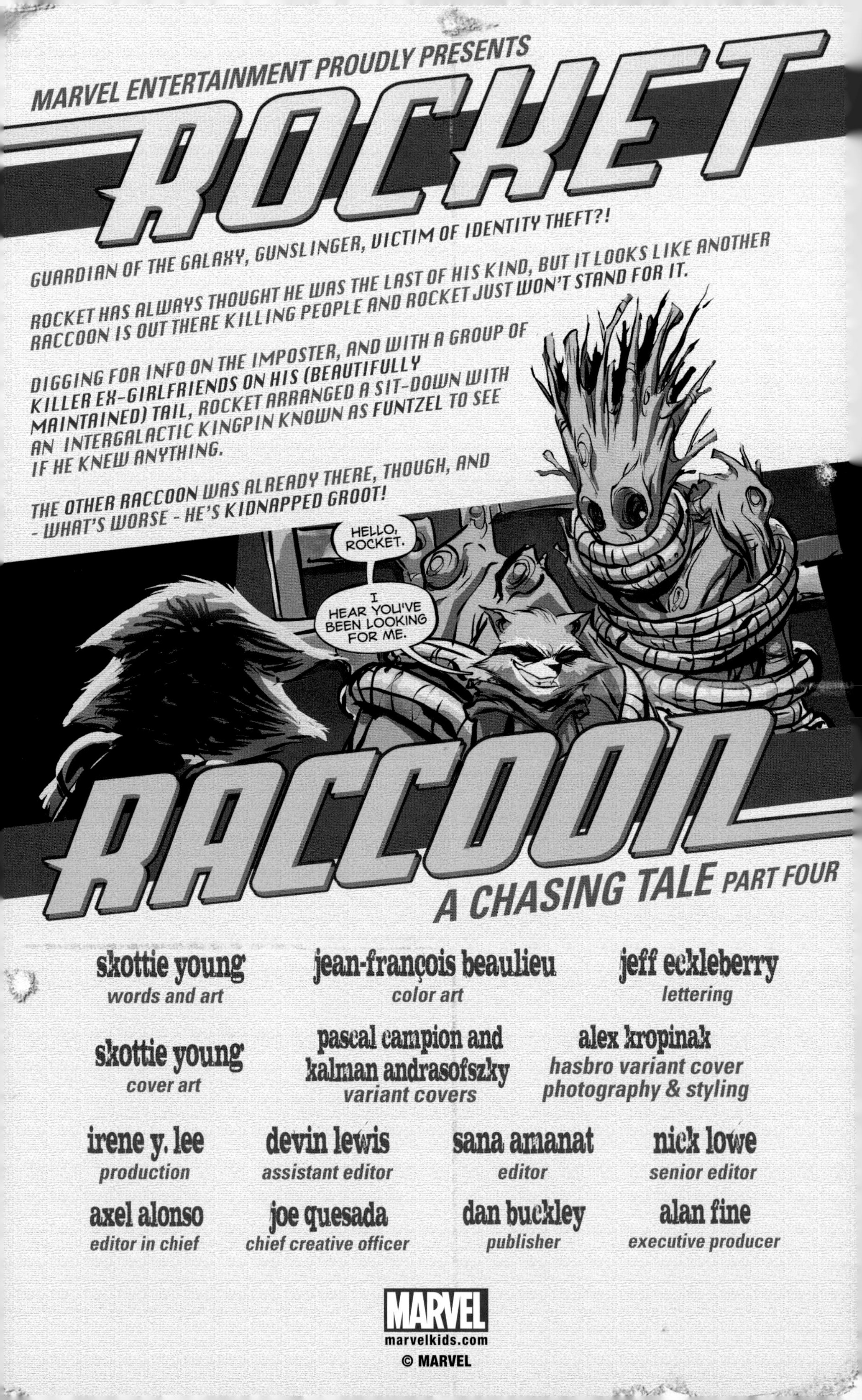
HELLO, ROCKET.
I HEAR YOU'VE BEEN LOOKING FOR ME.

# RACCOON

## A CHASING TALE PART FOUR

**skottie young**
*words and art*

**jean-françois beaulieu**
*color art*

**jeff eckleberry**
*lettering*

**skottie young**
*cover art*

**pascal campion and kalman andrasofszky**
*variant covers*

**alex kropinak**
*hasbro variant cover photography & styling*

**irene y. lee**
*production*

**devin lewis**
*assistant editor*

**sana amanat**
*editor*

**nick lowe**
*senior editor*

**axel alonso**
*editor in chief*

**joe quesada**
*chief creative officer*

**dan buckley**
*publisher*

**alan fine**
*executive producer*

MARVEL
marvelkids.com

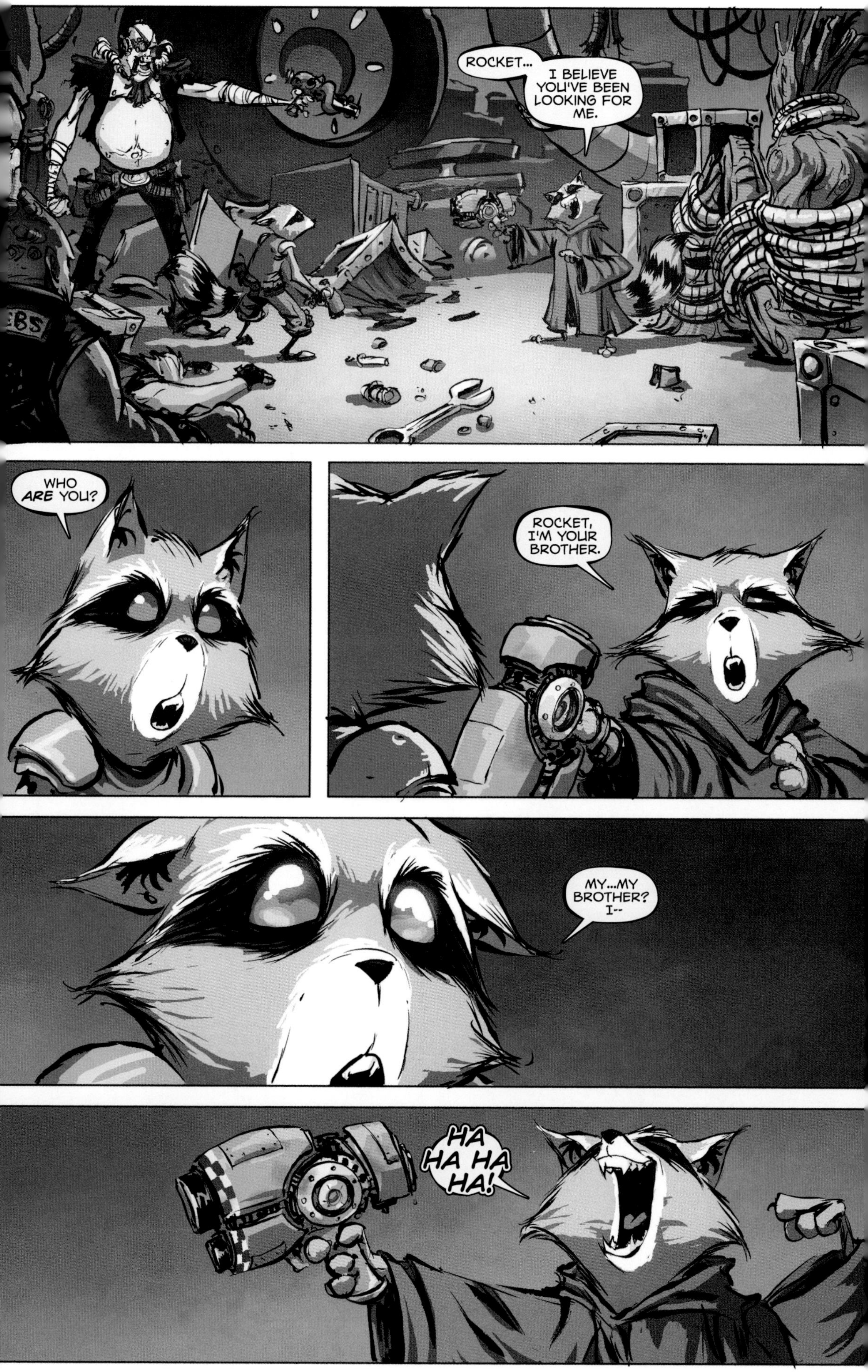
ROCKET...
I BELIEVE YOU'VE BEEN LOOKING FOR ME.
EBS
WHO ARE YOU?
ROCKET, I'M YOUR BROTHER.
MY...MY BROTHER? I--
HA HA HA HA!

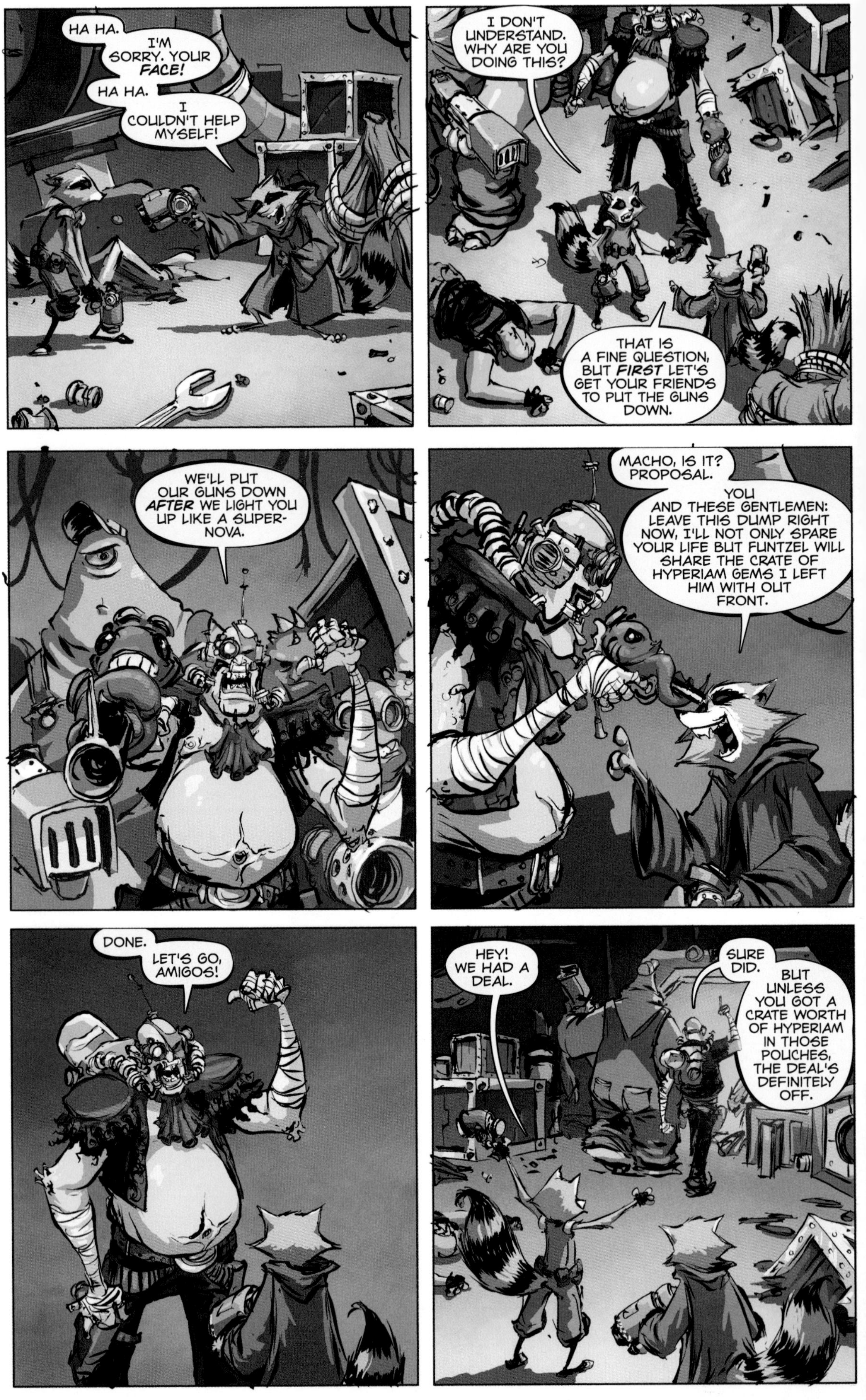
HA HA.
I'M SORRY. YOUR FACE!
HA HA.
I COULDN'T HELP MYSELF!
I DON'T UNDERSTAND. WHY ARE YOU DOING THIS?
THAT IS A FINE QUESTION, BUT FIRST LET'S GET YOUR FRIENDS TO PUT THE GUNS DOWN.
WE'LL PUT OUR GUNS DOWN AFTER WE LIGHT YOU UP LIKE A SUPER-NOVA.
MACHO, IS IT? PROPOSAL.
YOU AND THESE GENTLEMEN: LEAVE THIS DUMP RIGHT NOW, I'LL NOT ONLY SPARE YOUR LIFE BUT FUNTZEL WILL SHARE THE CRATE OF HYPERIAM GEMS I LEFT HIM WITH OUT FRONT.
DONE.
LET'S GO, AMIGOS!
HEY! WE HAD A DEAL.
SURE DID.
BUT UNLESS YOU GOT A CRATE WORTH OF HYPERIAM IN THOSE POUCHES, THE DEAL'S DEFINITELY OFF.

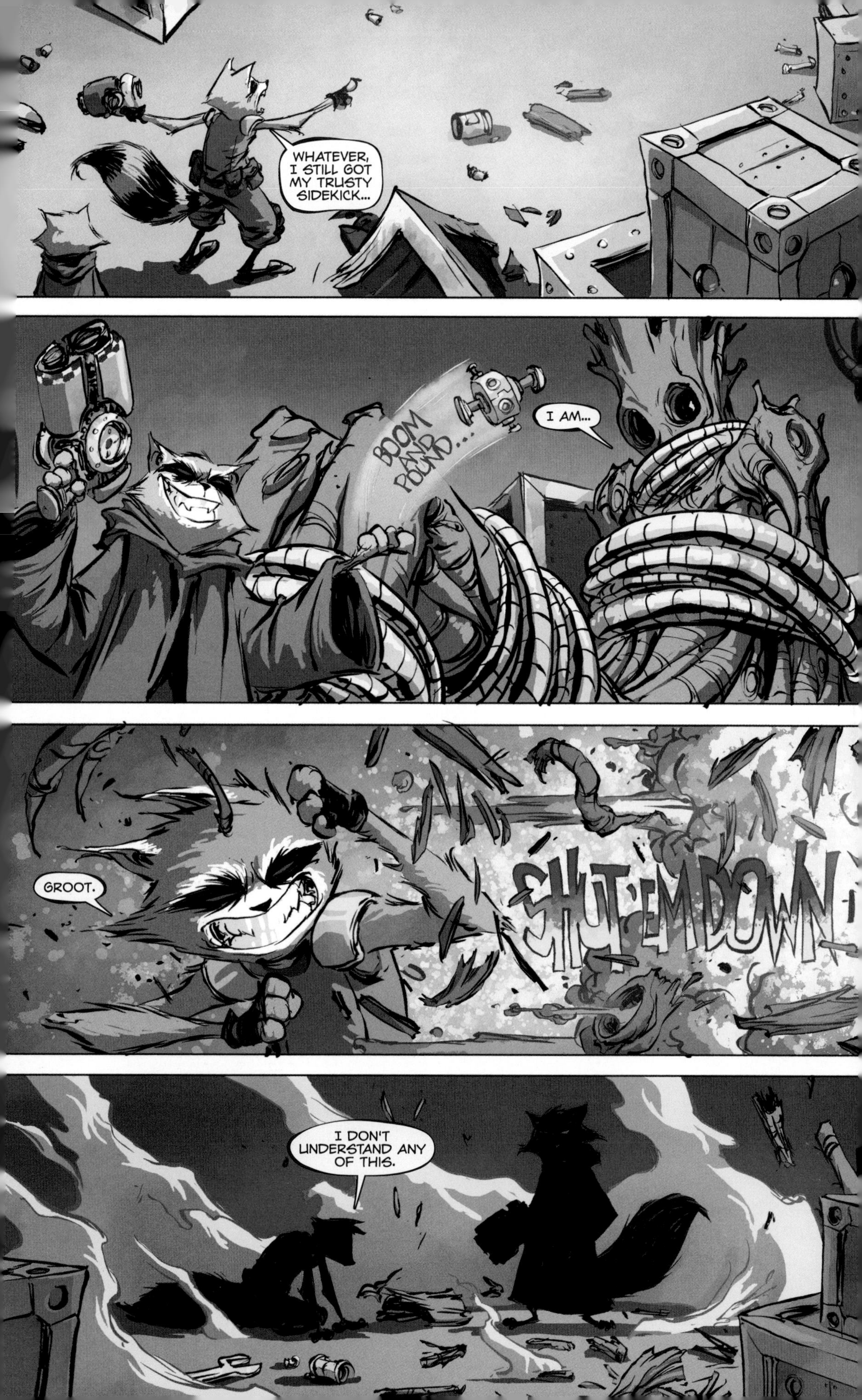
WHATEVER, I STILL GOT MY TRUSTY SIDEKICK...
BOOM AND POUND...
I AM...
GROOT.
SHUT'EM DOWN
I DON'T UNDERSTAND ANY OF THIS.

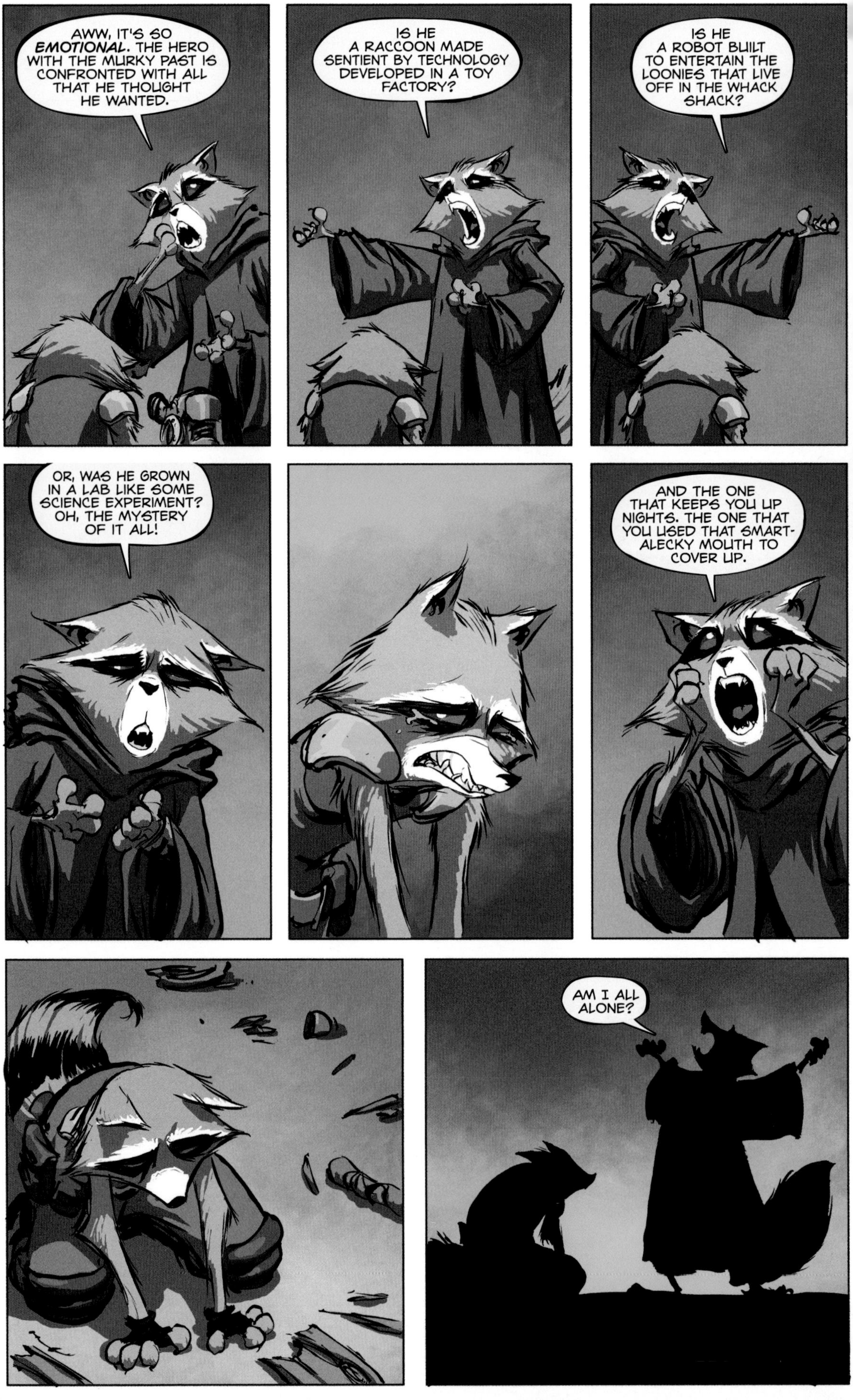
AWW, IT'S SO *EMOTIONAL*. THE HERO WITH THE MURKY PAST IS CONFRONTED WITH ALL THAT HE THOUGHT HE WANTED.
IS HE A RACCOON MADE SENTIENT BY TECHNOLOGY DEVELOPED IN A TOY FACTORY?
IS HE A ROBOT BUILT TO ENTERTAIN THE LOONIES THAT LIVE OFF IN THE WHACK SHACK?
OR, WAS HE GROWN IN A LAB LIKE SOME SCIENCE EXPERIMENT? OH, THE MYSTERY OF IT ALL!
AND THE ONE THAT KEEPS YOU UP NIGHTS. THE ONE THAT YOU USED THAT SMART-ALECKY MOUTH TO COVER UP.
AM I ALL ALONE?

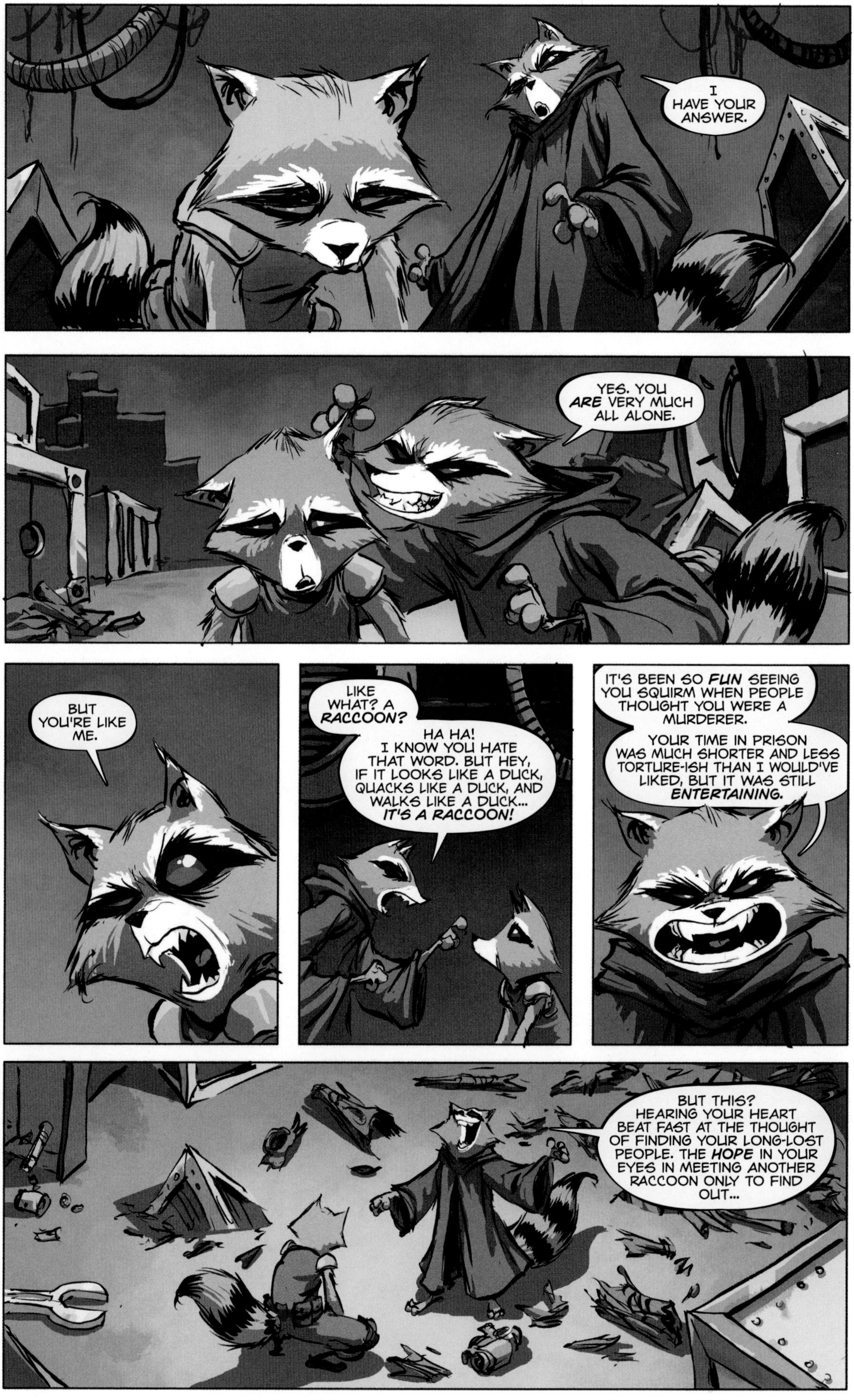
I HAVE YOUR ANSWER.
YES. YOU *ARE* VERY MUCH ALL ALONE.
BUT YOU'RE LIKE ME.
LIKE WHAT? A *RACCOON?*
HA HA! I KNOW YOU HATE THAT WORD. BUT HEY, IF IT LOOKS LIKE A DUCK, QUACKS LIKE A DUCK, AND WALKS LIKE A DUCK... *IT'S A RACCOON!*
IT'S BEEN SO *FUN* SEEING YOU SQUIRM WHEN PEOPLE THOUGHT YOU WERE A MURDERER.
YOUR TIME IN PRISON WAS MUCH SHORTER AND LESS TORTURE-ISH THAN I WOULD'VE LIKED, BUT IT WAS STILL *ENTERTAINING.*
BUT THIS? HEARING YOUR HEART BEAT FAST AT THE THOUGHT OF FINDING YOUR LONG-LOST PEOPLE. THE *HOPE* IN YOUR EYES IN MEETING ANOTHER RACCOON ONLY TO FIND OUT...

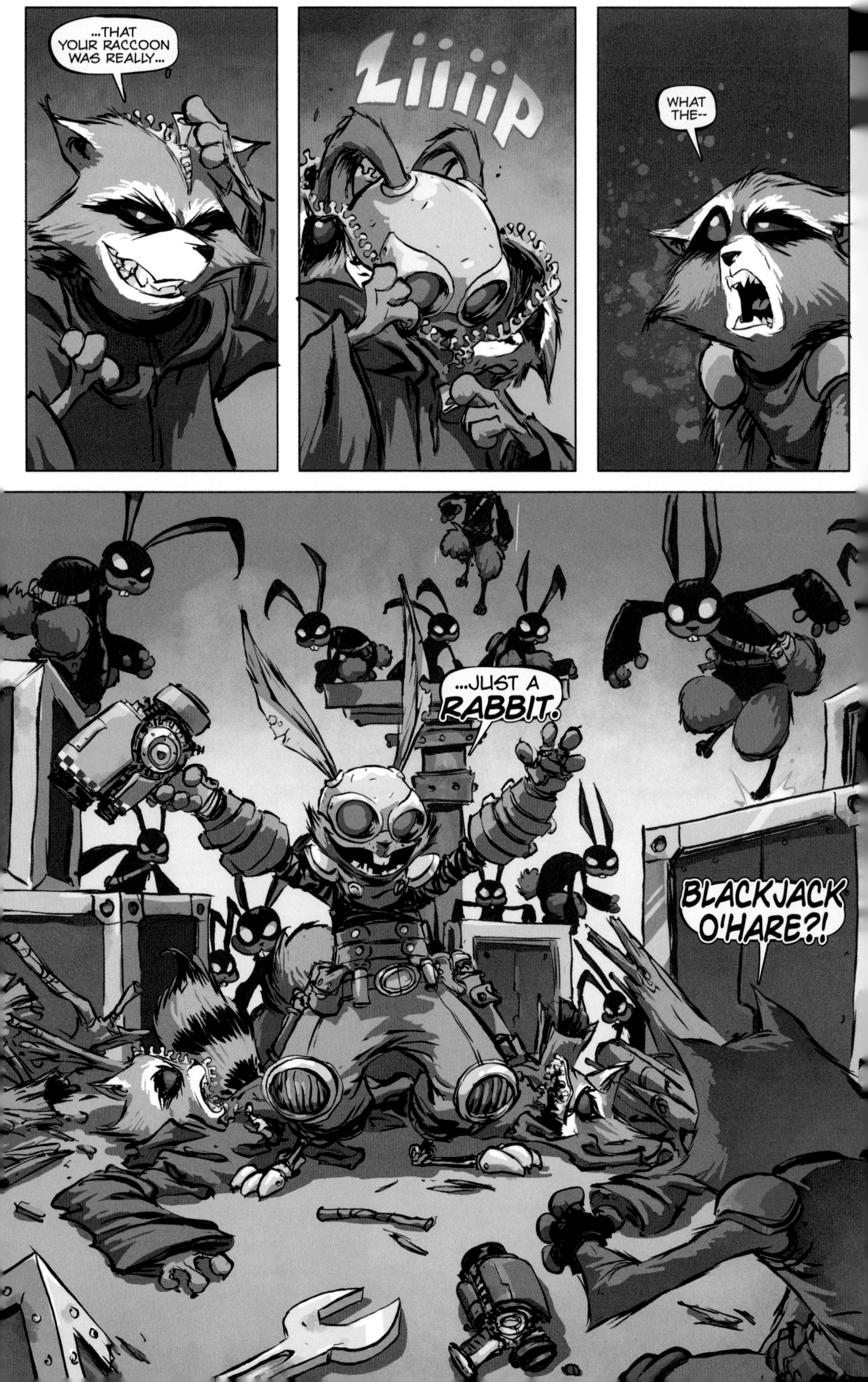
...THAT YOUR RACCOON WAS REALLY...
LIIIIP
WHAT THE--
...JUST A RABBIT.
BLACKJACK O'HARE?!

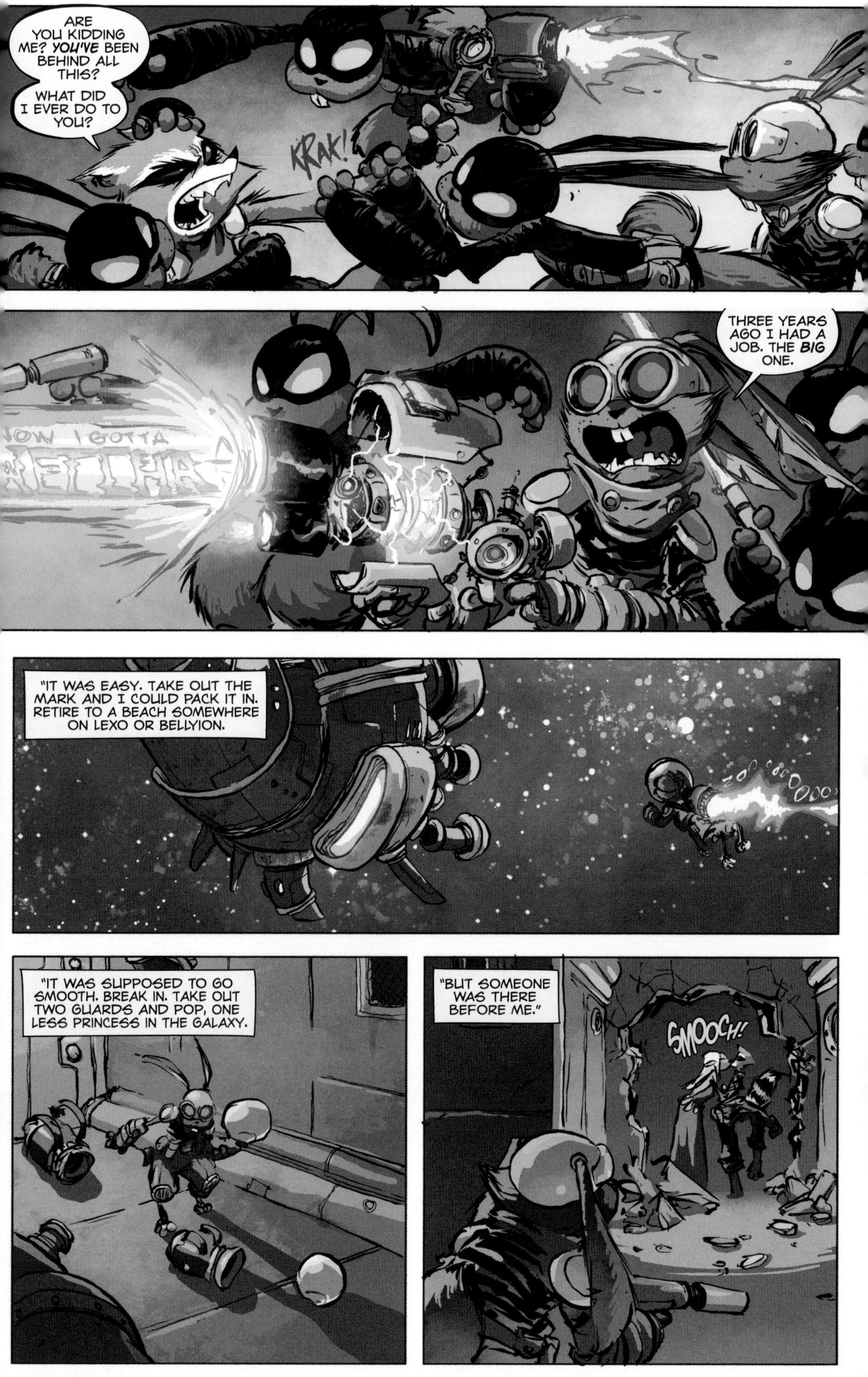
ARE YOU KIDDING ME? *YOU'VE* BEEN BEHIND ALL THIS?
WHAT DID I EVER DO TO YOU?
KRAK!
THREE YEARS AGO I HAD A JOB. THE *BIG* ONE.
"IT WAS EASY. TAKE OUT THE MARK AND I COULD PACK IT IN. RETIRE TO A BEACH SOMEWHERE ON LEXO OR BELLYION.
"IT WAS SUPPOSED TO GO SMOOTH. BREAK IN. TAKE OUT TWO GUARDS AND POP, ONE LESS PRINCESS IN THE GALAXY.
"BUT SOMEONE WAS THERE BEFORE ME."
SMOOCH!

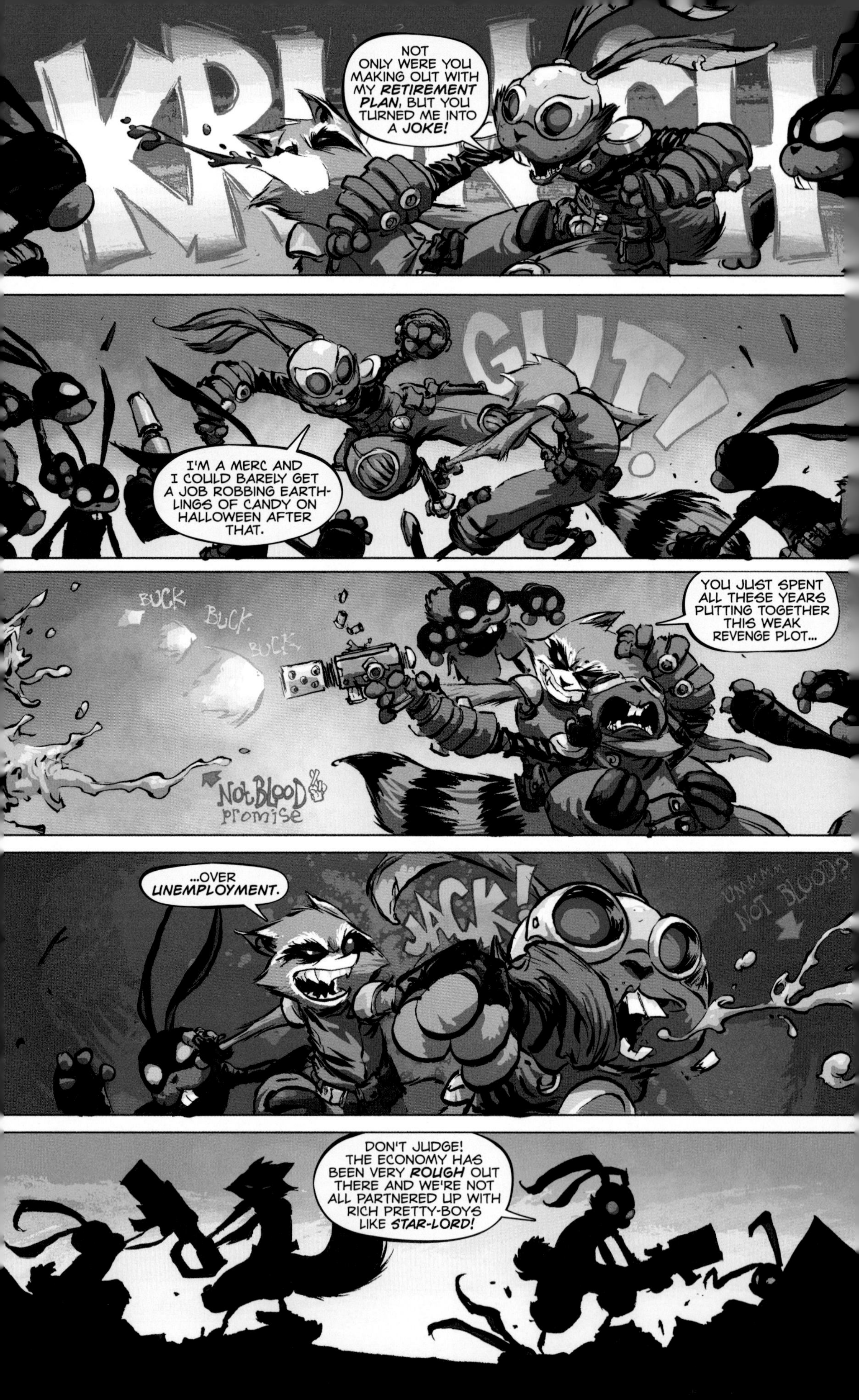
NOT ONLY WERE YOU MAKING OUT WITH MY *RETIREMENT PLAN*, BUT YOU TURNED ME INTO A *JOKE!*
GUT!
I'M A MERC AND I COULD BARELY GET A JOB ROBBING EARTHLINGS OF CANDY ON HALLOWEEN AFTER THAT.
BUCK
BUCK
BUCK
YOU JUST SPENT ALL THESE YEARS PUTTING TOGETHER THIS WEAK REVENGE PLOT...
Not Blood promise
...OVER *UNEMPLOYMENT*.
JACK!
UMMM... NOT BLOOD?
DON'T JUDGE! THE ECONOMY HAS BEEN VERY *ROUGH* OUT THERE AND WE'RE NOT ALL PARTNERED UP WITH RICH PRETTY-BOYS LIKE *STAR-LORD!*

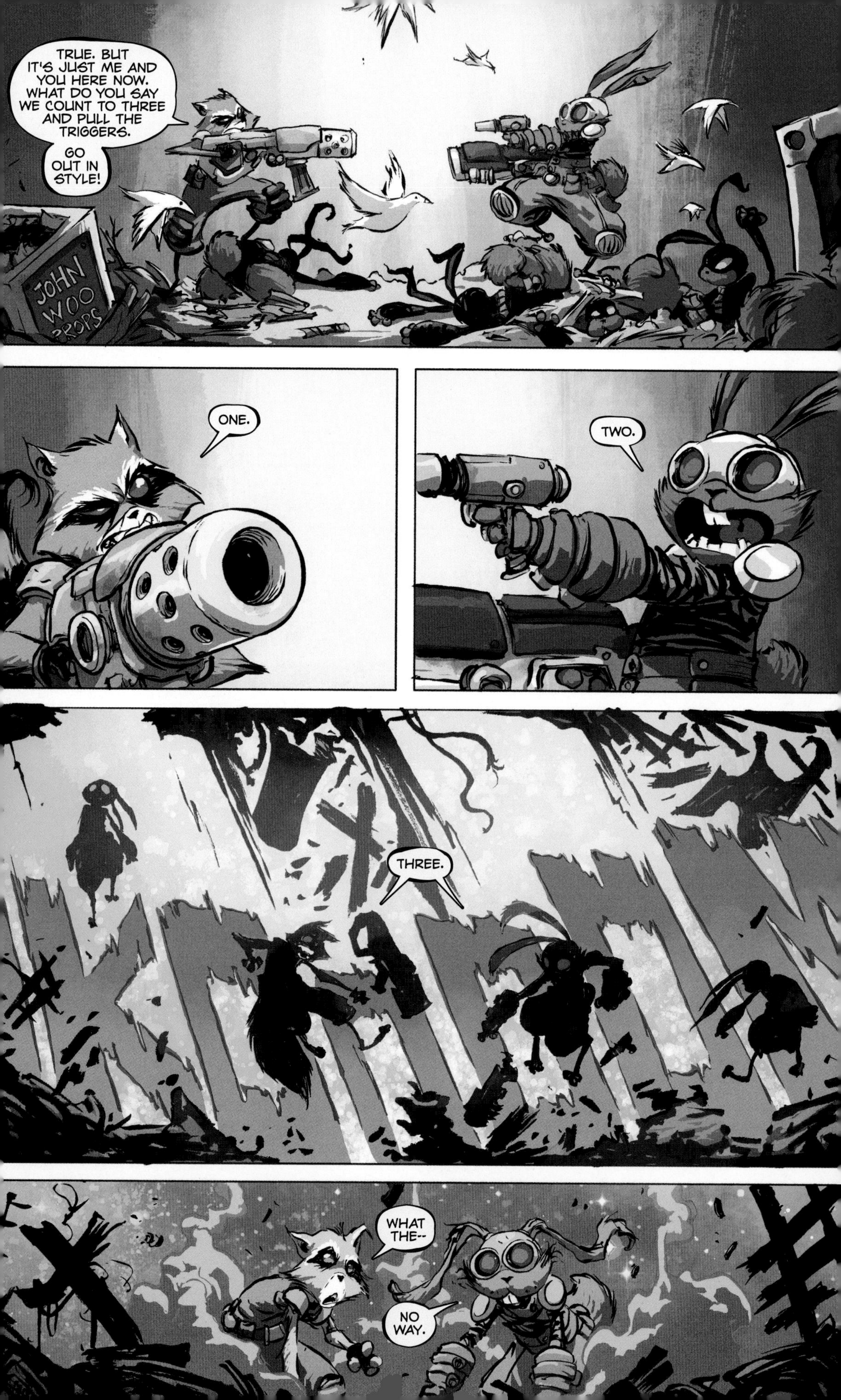
TRUE. BUT IT'S JUST ME AND YOU HERE NOW. WHAT DO YOU SAY WE COUNT TO THREE AND PULL THE TRIGGERS.
GO OUT IN STYLE!
JOHN WOO PROPS
ONE.
TWO.
THREE.
WHAT THE--
NO WAY.

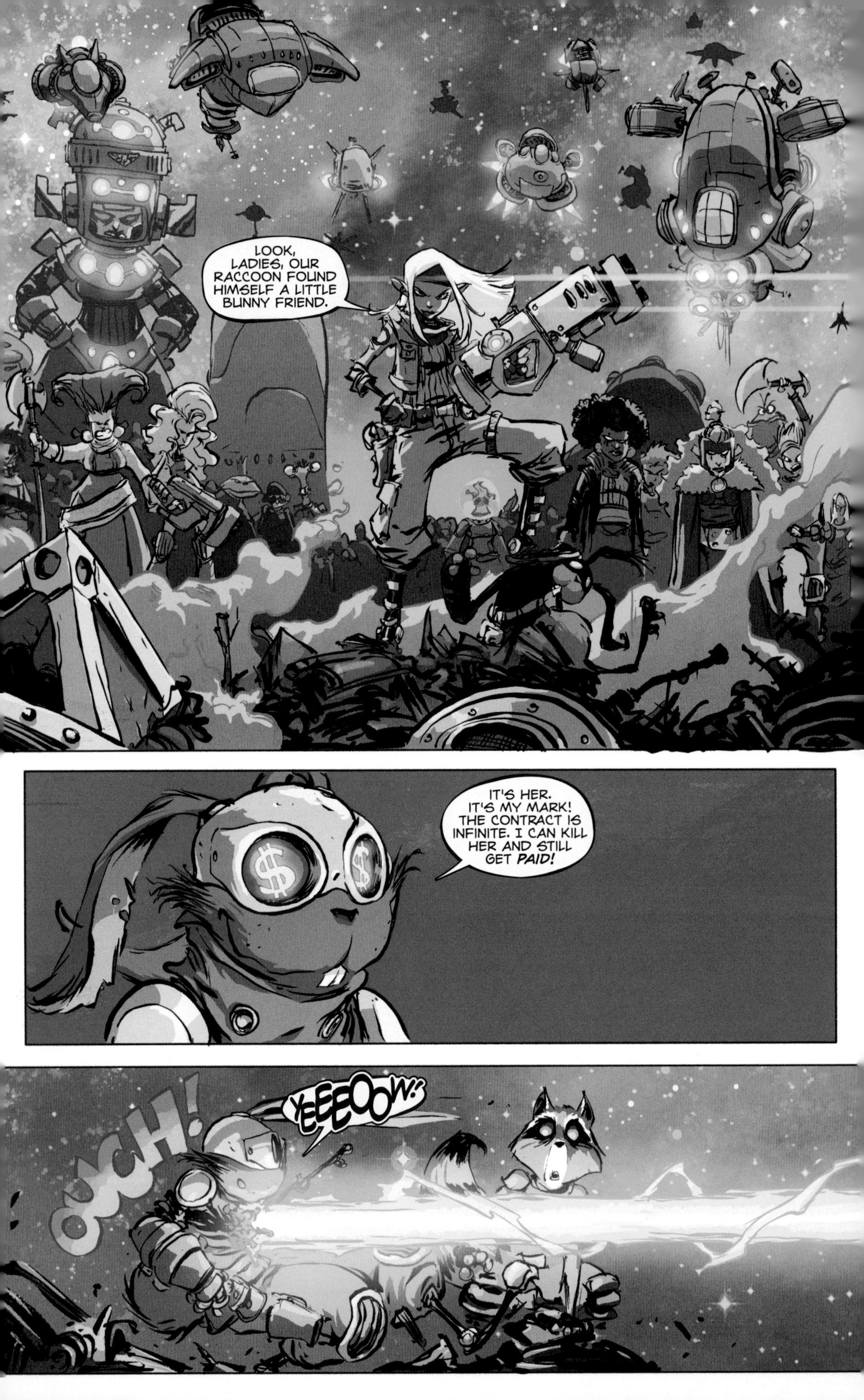
LOOK, LADIES, OUR RACCOON FOUND HIMSELF A LITTLE BUNNY FRIEND.
IT'S HER. IT'S MY MARK! THE CONTRACT IS INFINITE. I CAN KILL HER AND STILL GET *PAID!*
OUCH!
YEEEOOW!

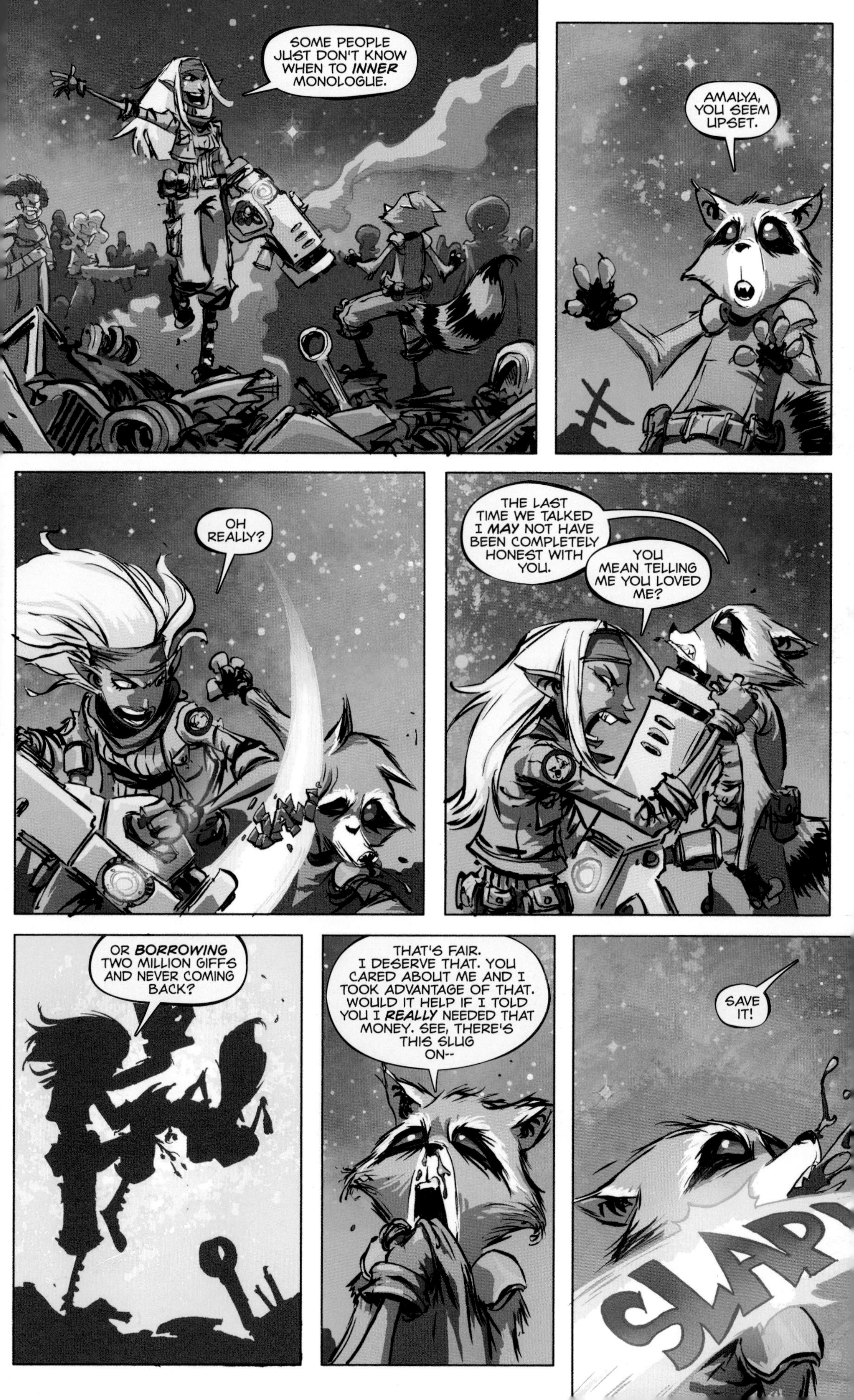
SOME PEOPLE JUST DON'T KNOW WHEN TO *INNER* MONOLOGUE.
AMALYA, YOU SEEM UPSET.
OH REALLY?
THE LAST TIME WE TALKED I *MAY* NOT HAVE BEEN COMPLETELY HONEST WITH YOU.
YOU MEAN TELLING ME YOU LOVED ME?
OR *BORROWING* TWO MILLION GIFFS AND NEVER COMING BACK?
THAT'S FAIR. I DESERVE THAT. YOU CARED ABOUT ME AND I TOOK ADVANTAGE OF THAT. WOULD IT HELP IF I TOLD YOU I *REALLY* NEEDED THAT MONEY. SEE, THERE'S THIS SLUG ON--
SAVE IT!

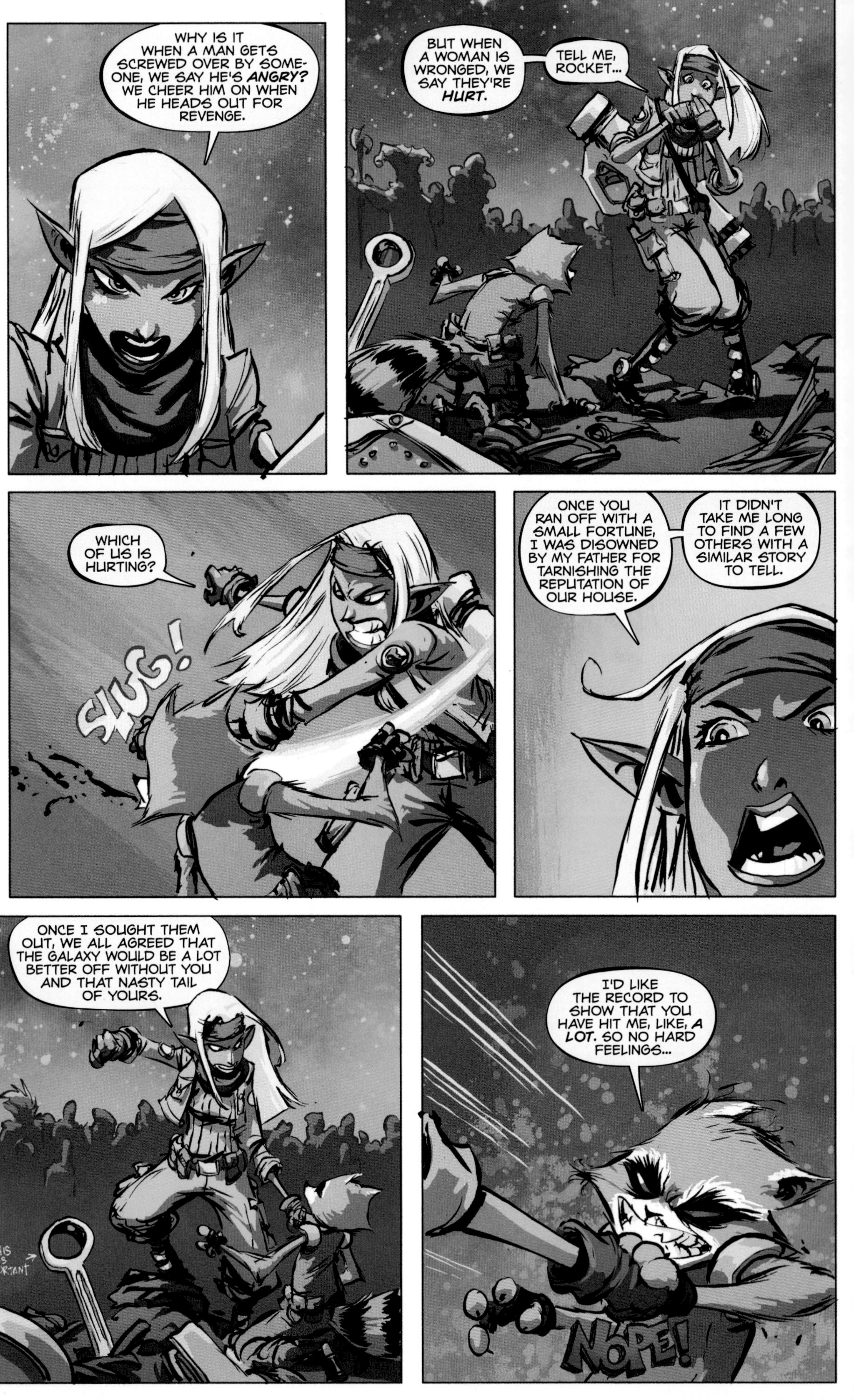
WHY IS IT WHEN A MAN GETS SCREWED OVER BY SOME-ONE, WE SAY HE'S *ANGRY?* WE CHEER HIM ON WHEN HE HEADS OUT FOR REVENGE.
BUT WHEN A WOMAN IS WRONGED, WE SAY THEY'RE *HURT*.
TELL ME, ROCKET...
WHICH OF US IS HURTING?
SLUG!
ONCE YOU RAN OFF WITH A SMALL FORTUNE, I WAS DISOWNED BY MY FATHER FOR TARNISHING THE REPUTATION OF OUR HOUSE.
IT DIDN'T TAKE ME LONG TO FIND A FEW OTHERS WITH A SIMILAR STORY TO TELL.
ONCE I SOUGHT THEM OUT, WE ALL AGREED THAT THE GALAXY WOULD BE A LOT BETTER OFF WITHOUT YOU AND THAT NASTY TAIL OF YOURS.
THIS IS
I'D LIKE THE RECORD TO SHOW THAT YOU HAVE HIT ME, LIKE, *A LOT*. SO NO HARD FEELINGS...
NOPE!

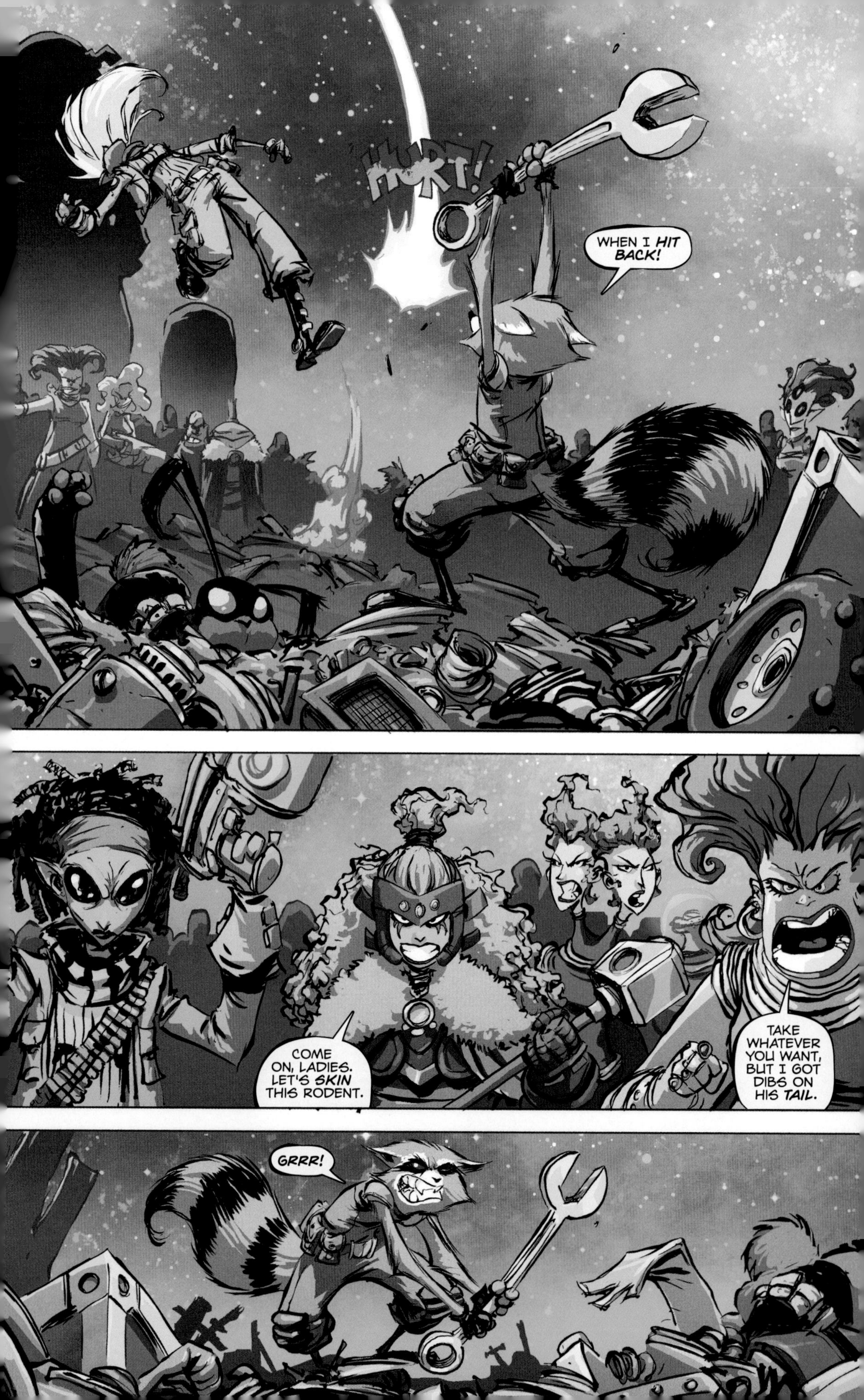
HURT!
WHEN I HIT BACK!
COME ON, LADIES. LET'S SKIN THIS RODENT.
TAKE WHATEVER YOU WANT, BUT I GOT DIBS ON HIS TAIL.
GRRR!

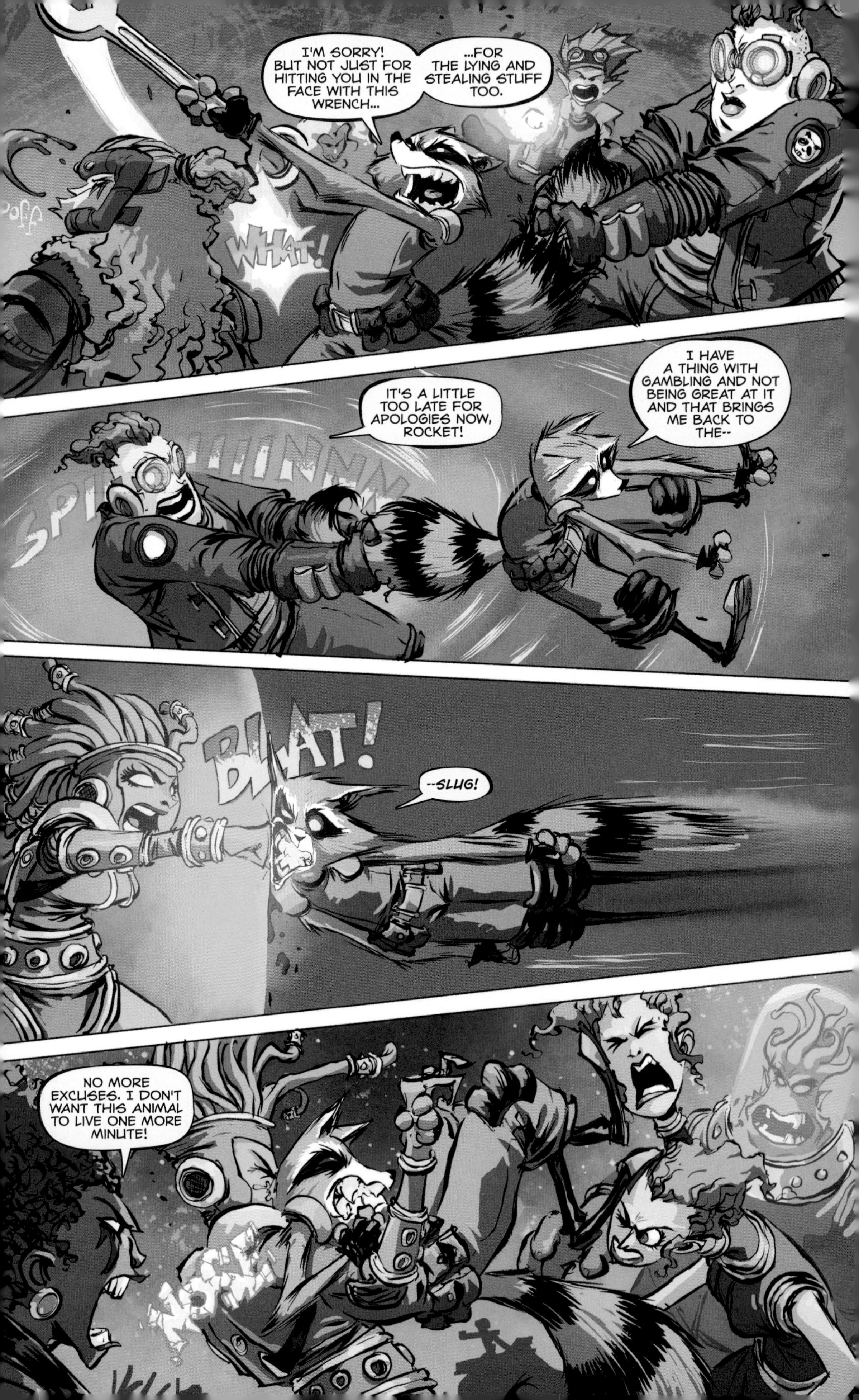
I'M SORRY! BUT NOT JUST FOR HITTING YOU IN THE FACE WITH THIS WRENCH...
...FOR THE LYING AND STEALING STUFF TOO.
WHAT!
IT'S A LITTLE TOO LATE FOR APOLOGIES NOW, ROCKET!
I HAVE A THING WITH GAMBLING AND NOT BEING GREAT AT IT AND THAT BRINGS ME BACK TO THE--
--SLUG!
NO MORE EXCUSES. I DON'T WANT THIS ANIMAL TO LIVE ONE MORE MINUTE!

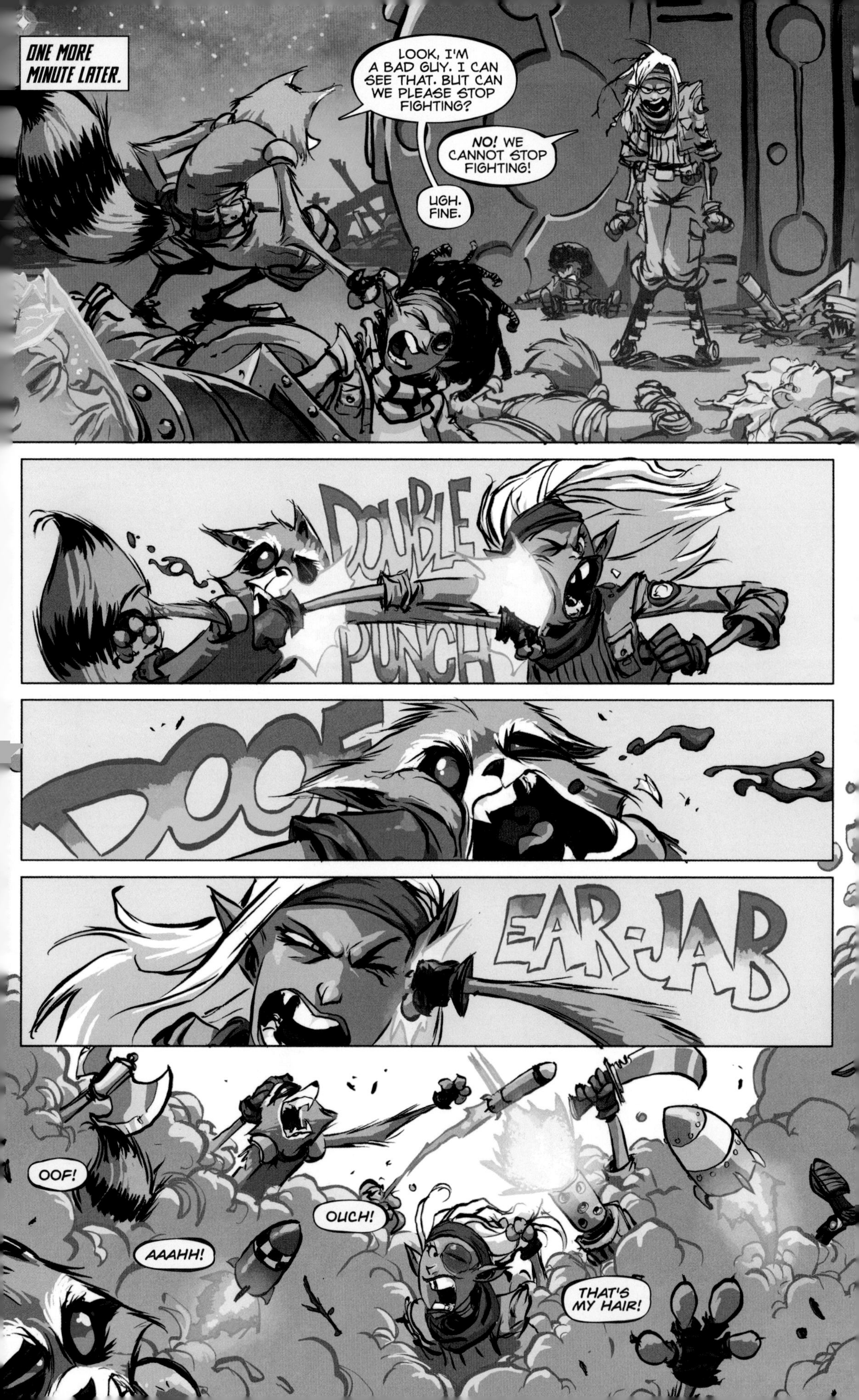
ONE MORE MINUTE LATER.
LOOK, I'M A BAD GUY. I CAN SEE THAT. BUT CAN WE PLEASE STOP FIGHTING?
NO! WE CANNOT STOP FIGHTING!
UGH. FINE.
DOUBLE PUNCH
EAR-JAB
OOF!
OUCH!
AAAHH!
THAT'S MY HAIR!

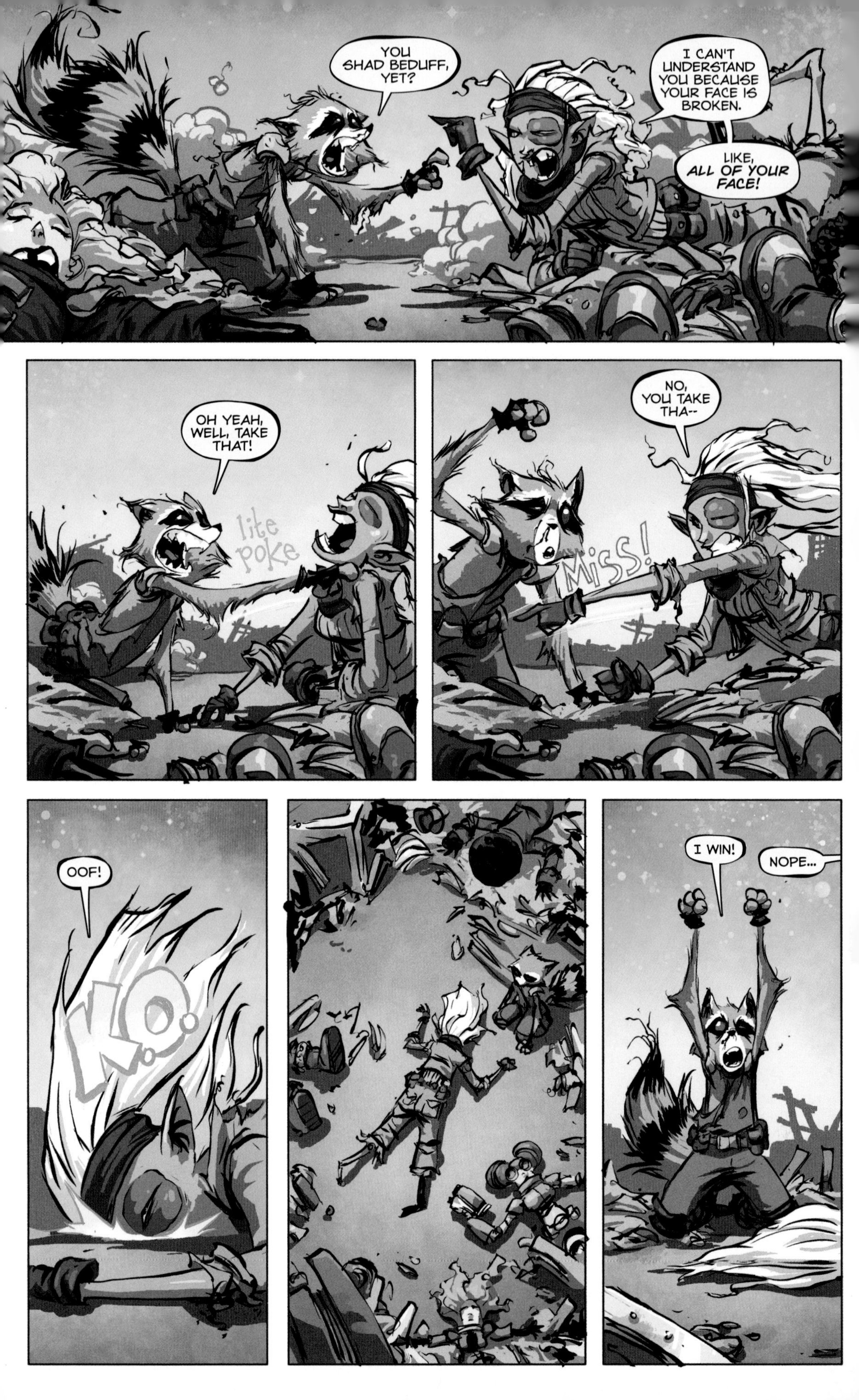
YOU SHAD BEDUFF, YET?
I CAN'T UNDERSTAND YOU BECAUSE YOUR FACE IS BROKEN.
LIKE, ALL OF YOUR FACE!
OH YEAH, WELL, TAKE THAT!
lite poke
NO, YOU TAKE THA--
MISS!
OOF!
I WIN!
NOPE...

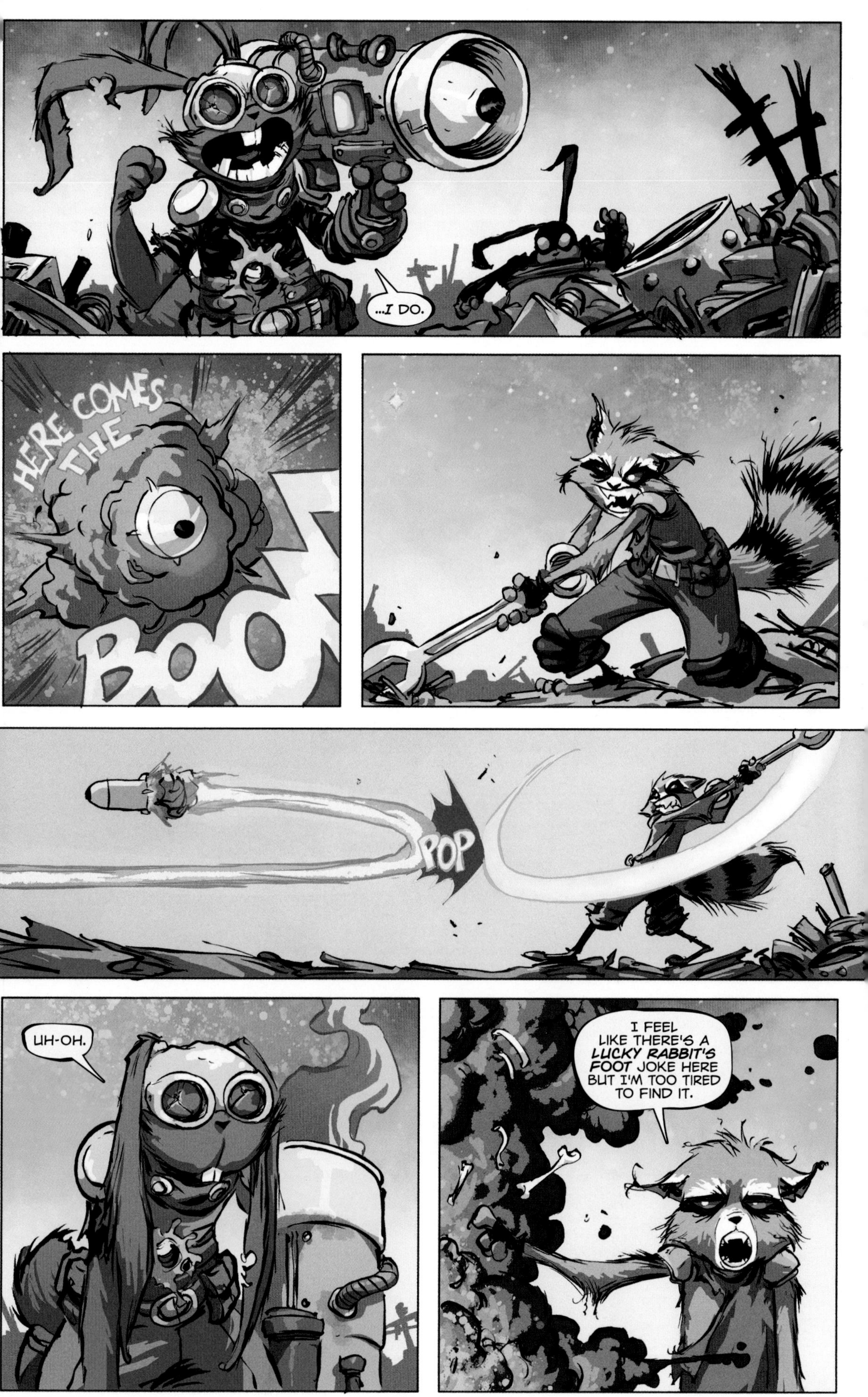
...I DO.
HERE COMES THE
BOO
POP
UH-OH.
I FEEL LIKE THERE'S A LUCKY RABBIT'S FOOT JOKE HERE BUT I'M TOO TIRED TO FIND IT.

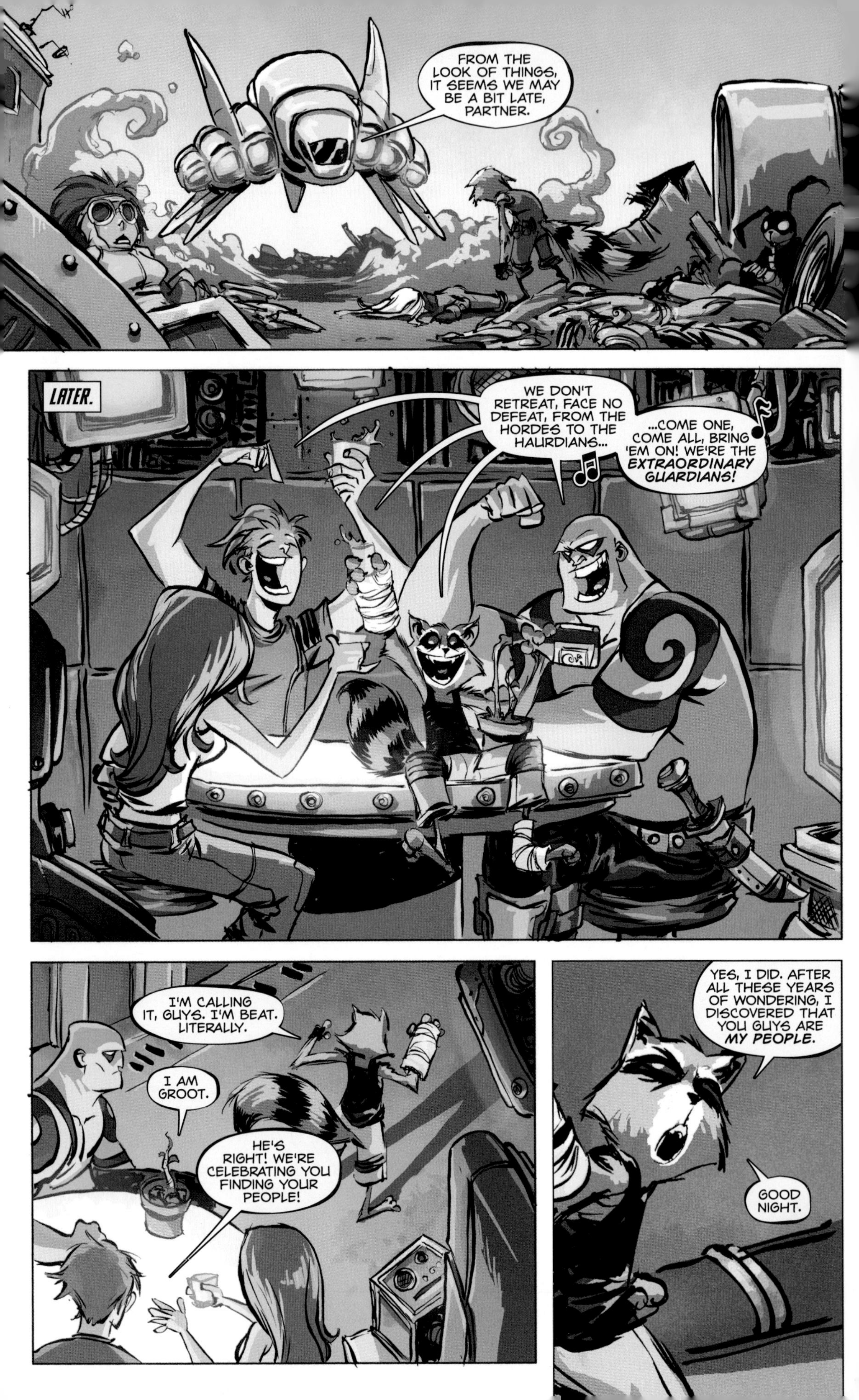
FROM THE LOOK OF THINGS, IT SEEMS WE MAY BE A BIT LATE, PARTNER.
LATER.
WE DON'T RETREAT, FACE NO DEFEAT, FROM THE HORDES TO THE HAURDIANS...
...COME ONE, COME ALL, BRING 'EM ON! WE'RE THE EXTRAORDINARY GUARDIANS!
I'M CALLING IT, GUYS. I'M BEAT. LITERALLY.
I AM GROOT.
HE'S RIGHT! WE'RE CELEBRATING YOU FINDING YOUR PEOPLE!
YES, I DID. AFTER ALL THESE YEARS OF WONDERING, I DISCOVERED THAT YOU GUYS ARE MY PEOPLE.
GOOD NIGHT.

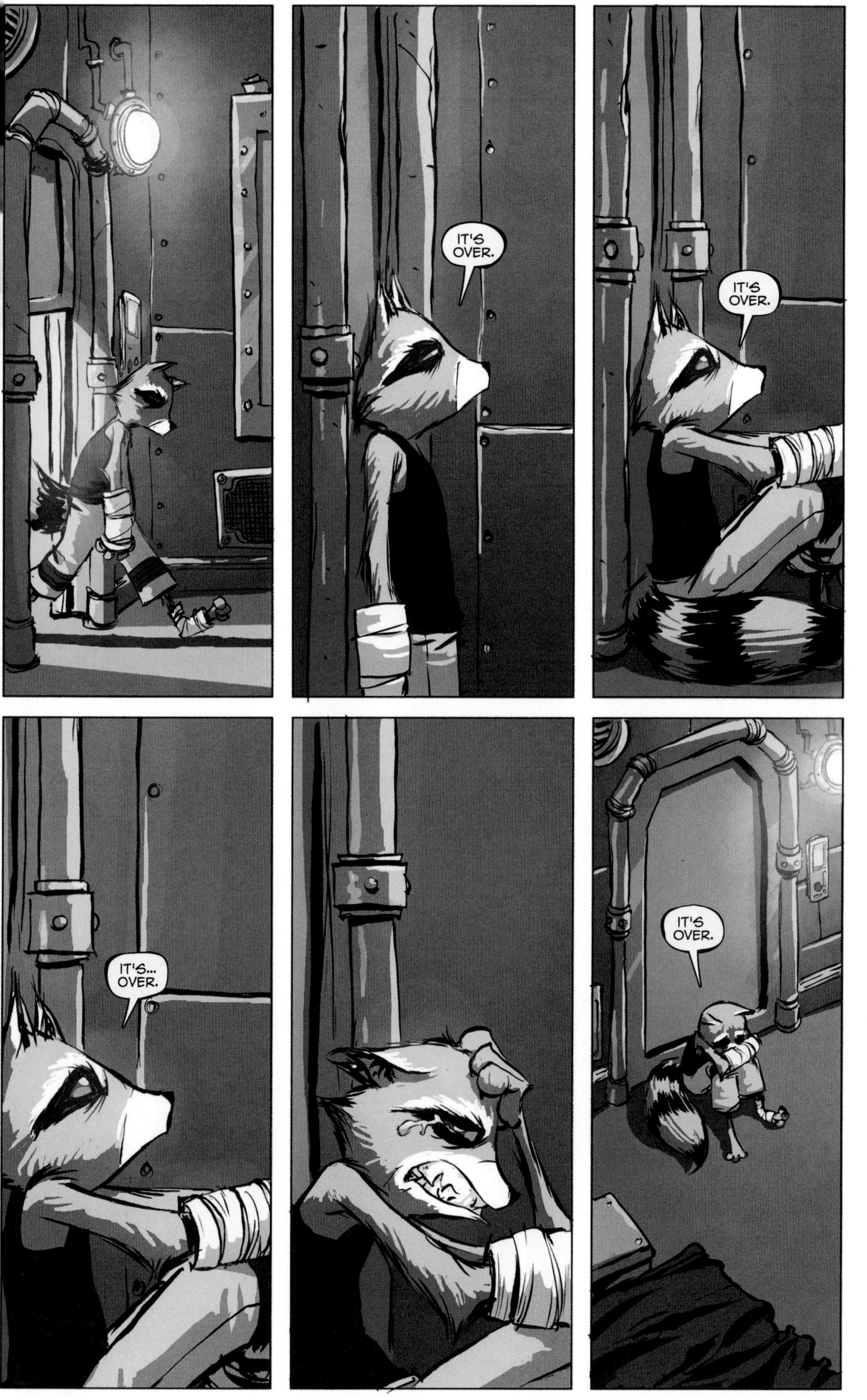

IT'S OVER.
IT'S OVER.
IT'S... OVER.
IT'S OVER.

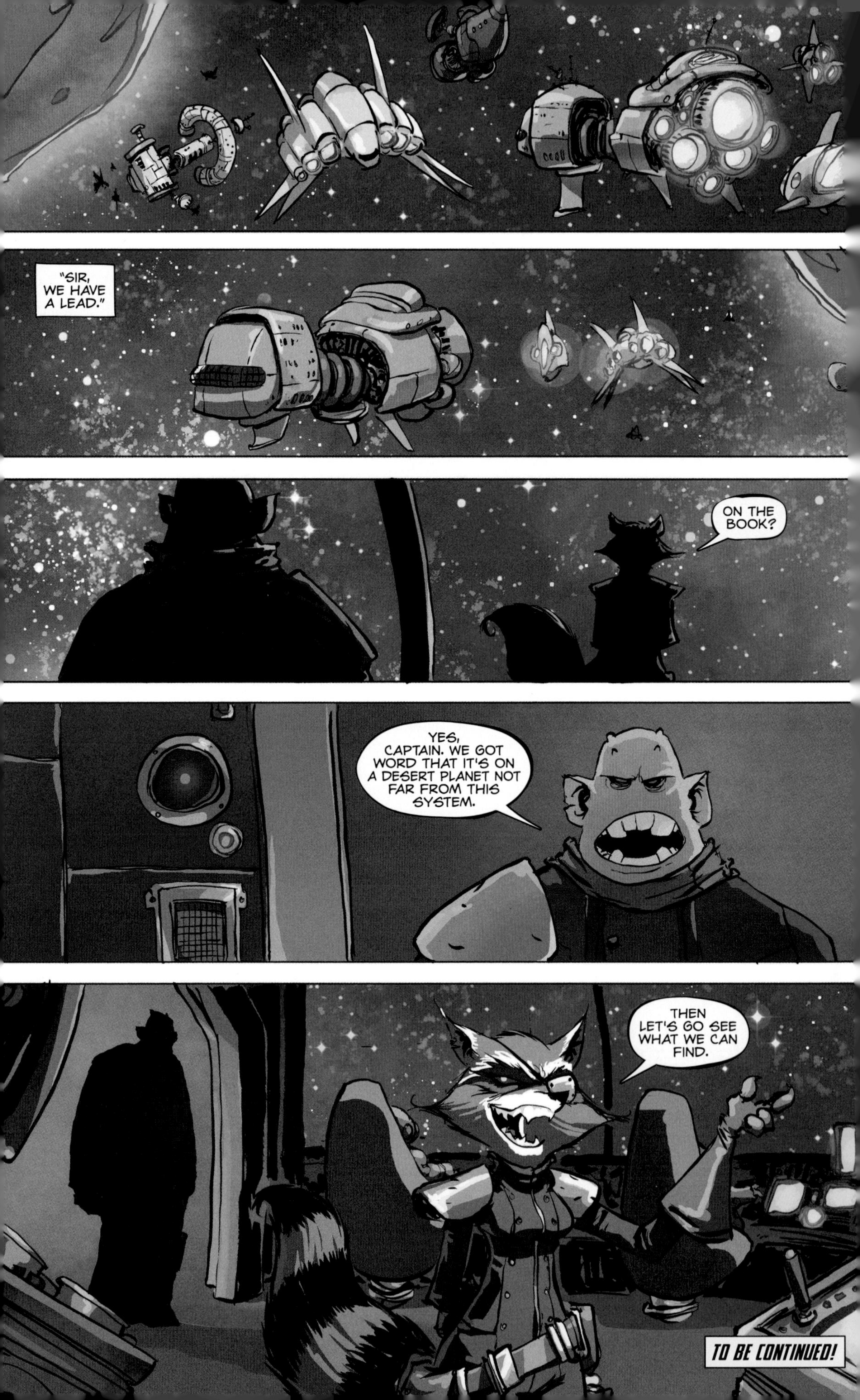
"SIR, WE HAVE A LEAD."
ON THE BOOK?
YES, CAPTAIN. WE GOT WORD THAT IT'S ON A DESERT PLANET NOT FAR FROM THIS SYSTEM.
THEN LET'S GO SEE WHAT WE CAN FIND.
TO BE CONTINUED!